Thumbelina

Once upon a time, there was a kind woman who wished for a tiny daughter, but she had no idea where to find one. She decided to visit a fairy and ask for her help.

"Here is a magical grain of barley," said the fairy. "It is no ordinary seed. Plant this in a flowerpot and see what happens."

2

The woman thanked the fairy, and went home and planted the seed. Before long, the seed grew into a large, beautiful flower, but its petals remained tightly closed.

"What a lovely flower!" the woman exclaimed, and she kissed the bud.

With the kiss, the bud popped opened, revealing a tiny girl. She was the smallest and loveliest girl that the woman had ever seen! She was barely as big as a thumb, and so she was named Thumbelina.

The woman loved Thumbelina very much, and treated her like a daughter. Thumbelina slept in a walnut shell bed, with a mattress made of violet petals and a rose petal as a blanket.

One night, a big, slimy toad crept in through the window and onto the table where Thumbelina slept.

"Why, she'll make the perfect wife for my son!" croaked the toad. With that, she grabbed Thumbelina and her walnut shell bed, and hopped out the window and down the garden path.

4

The old toad brought Thumbelina to the muddy riverbank where she lived with her son. He was just as ugly as his mother, and could only croak at the tiny sleeping girl.

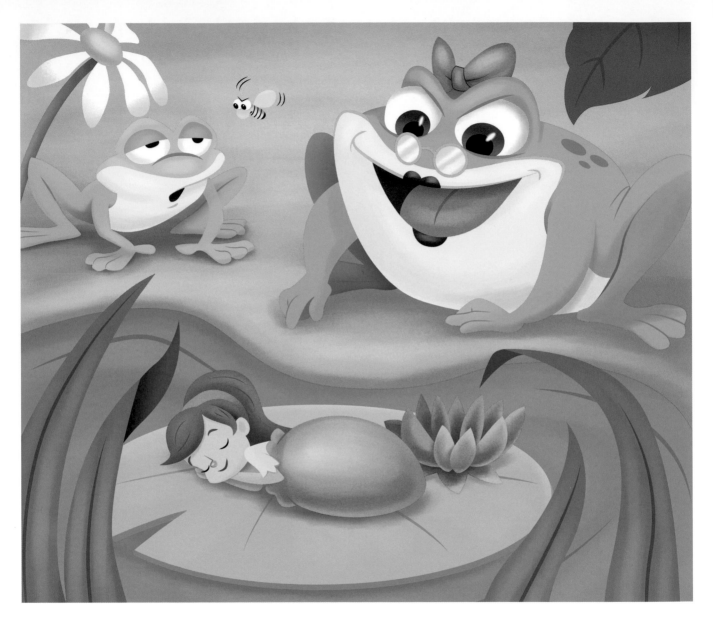

"Stop croaking," said the mother toad, "or you'll wake her.
Let's put her on a big lily pad in the middle of the river while we
tidy up."

When Thumbelina woke the next morning, she found herself surrounded by water. She had no way to reach the shore! Thumbelina sat down on the lily pad and cried. Before long, the old toad swam out to the lily pad.

"Soon you shall meet my son," said the toad. "He is going to be your husband. You'll live with us on the riverbank!"

Poor Thumbelina didn't want to marry a toad! She cried and cried, and the fish in the river poked their heads up to see what was wrong. The fish agreed that sweet Thumbelina should not marry a horrid toad, and so they chewed through the stem of the lily pad. Once it was freed, the lily pad floated downstream, taking Thumbelina far away from the toads.

As Thumbelina sailed down the river, the birds in the bushes chirped excitedly.

"What a pretty girl!" they twittered.

Just then, a large beetle flew by and snatched her off the lily pad.

The beetle carried Thumbelina to a tree and placed her on a soft leaf. He fetched some honey for her to eat, and told her how pretty she was, even if she didn't look at all like a beetle.

After a while, other beetles came to visit. All the lady beetles giggled at Thumbelina—she only had two legs, and no antennae! They thought she looked quite silly.

Since the lady beetles kept calling Thumbelina ugly, the beetle who had snatched her soon agreed. He brought Thumbelina down from the tree and left her on a daisy. Poor Thumbelina wept because the beetles had teased her so much, but she was really just as lovely as ever.

All summer long, Thumbelina lived in the woods with only the
singing birds to keep her company. She wove a bed from blades
of grass, and placed it under a large leaf to protect her from the rain.
She ate nectar from the flowers, and drank dew from their leaves.

When winter came, the plants withered away and the birds flew off to warmer places. Poor Thumbelina was terribly cold and alone, so she set out to find some shelter. At the edge of the woods, Thumbelina saw a small door. She knocked on it, and was greeted by a field mouse.

"Oh, you poor girl!" exclaimed the mouse. "You must be frozen. Come inside, where it is cozy and warm."

The kind field mouse quite liked Thumbelina, and invited the tiny girl to live with her. Thumbelina helped the mouse cook and clean, and told her stories of her adventures.

"My neighbor is coming to visit," said the mouse one day. "His house is even nicer than mine, and he has all the food he could ever need. If you're lucky, he might want to be your husband. Then he will take care of you!"

That evening, the neighbor came over. Thumbelina was surprised to see that he was a mole! He talked quite a lot, but had nothing nice to say about the sun or flowers as he had never seen them. In fact, he hoped it would be a long winter as he quite liked the cold.

After dinner, the mouse asked Thumbelina to sing, and the mole fell in love with her as soon as he heard her lovely voice. The mole invited Thumbelina and the field mouse to visit his house, and led them through a new tunnel that he had just finished digging.

As they walked, they saw a beautiful swallow lying dead on the ground in the mole's tunnel.

"Thank goodness I was not born a bird," said the mole. "Nothing could be worse! All they do is chirp all summer, and when winter comes, they become so cold that they drop out of the sky."

Thumbelina felt sad as she looked at the bird. *Maybe he is one of the birds who sang to me all summer,* she thought. *What joy he brought me!*

That night, Thumbelina couldn't sleep. She kept thinking about the bird, cold and alone. She got out of bed, gathered some leaves, and carried them quietly down the tunnel. When she reached the swallow, she stroked his feathers, and then gently placed the leaves around him.

"Farewell, beautiful bird," said Thumbelina. "Thank you for your summer songs."

Thumbelina laid her head on the bird's chest, but was quite startled when she heard a thumping noise. It turned out to be the swallow's heart—he was still alive, only numb with cold! Now that he was warming up, he was returning to life.

The next night, Thumbelina returned to the bird. He was awake now, but still weak.

"Thank you for helping me," said the swallow. "I feel so nice and warm again. Soon I'll be strong enough to fly back into the warm sunshine."

"It's still cold outside," Thumbelina replied. "Just stay here and I'll take good care of you."

The swallow told Thumbelina that he had torn his wing on a thorn and couldn't keep up with the other birds when they flew off to a warmer spot. That was all he could remember, and didn't know how he had ended up in the tunnel.

The swallow stayed underground all winter long. Thumbelina took good care of him, and was happy that the mole and the field mouse ignored the bird.

When spring arrived, Thumbelina helped the swallow outside. As he flapped his wings, the swallow asked Thumbelina to join him on his journey.

"I'm flying away to a warmer country, where the sun always shines," said the swallow. "Will you come with me?"

Thumbelina agreed, and called goodbye to the field mouse. She climbed onto the swallow's back, and he rose into the air.

They flew over forests, lakes, and mountains. At last they reached the warm country, where the fields were full of lush flowers, and butterflies fluttered from blossom to blossom.

The swallow brought Thumbelina to the tall tree where he had his nest. Beneath the tree was a cluster of lovely white flowers. The swallow gently placed Thumbelina on the petals of the largest blossom. There, in the middle of the flower, was a tiny man, just the same size as Thumbelina. He had a gold crown on his head and delicate wings at his shoulders. In every flower was a tiny man or woman just like him, and he was the king of them all.

The king was the most handsome man Thumbelina had ever seen! Likewise, the king thought Thumbelina was the loveliest girl in the world, and he placed his crown on her head. He asked Thumbelina to be his wife, the queen of all the flowers.

He was certainly a different sort of husband than a toad or a mole! He was just like Thumbelina, and so Thumbelina said yes to the handsome king.

The little lords and ladies from the other flowers came to meet
Thumbelina. Each brought a present for the new queen, but the best
was a pair of beautiful wings. They were fastened to Thumbelina's
shoulders so she could fly from flower to flower. The swallow sang
a happy song, and they all lived happily ever after.

PISTOL PACKIN' MADAMS

"Hard workin', hard livin', and hard lovin', these pistol-packin' madams were the brave and colorful business women of the Old West. What an inspiration. . . ."

—Kim Dickens, *Deadwood*'s Joanie Stubbs